PRAIRIE FRIENDS

by Nancy Smiler Levinson

pictures by Stacey Schuett

HarperCollins*Publishers*

For Anne Hoppe, who shared my vision of a prairie story,

and Marianne Wallace, who helped the lost friends find their way

—N.S.L.

For Sofia, who knows the value of a good friend

—S.S.

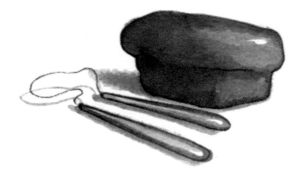

HarperCollins®, 🐎®, and I Can Read Book® are
trademarks of HarperCollins Publishers Inc.

Prairie Friends
Text copyright © 2003 by Nancy Smiler Levinson
Illustrations copyright © 2003 by Stacey Schuett
Printed in the U.S.A. All rights reserved.
www.harperchildrens.com

Library of Congress Cataloging-in-Publication Data
Levinson, Nancy Smiler.
    Prairie friends / story by Nancy Smiler Levinson ; pictures by Stacey Schuett.
        p.   cm. — (An I can read book)
    "An I can read book."
    Summary: When Betsy learns that a new family is coming to the Nebraska prairie, she
hopes they have a daughter who will be her friend.
    ISBN 0-06-028001-8 — ISBN 0-06-028002-6 (lib. bdg.) — ISBN 0-06-000856-3 (pbk.)
    [1. Friendship—Fiction.   2. Frontier and pioneer life—Nebraska—Fiction.
3. Nebraska—History—Fiction.]   I. Schuett, Stacey, ill.   II. Title.   III. Series.
PZ7.L5794 Pr   2003   2002020538
[E]—dc21

❖

Contents

Chapter 1 ❧ The Husking Bee

It was the end of summer

on the Nebraska prairie.

A gentle wind

blew across the wide, open land.

"This is a good day

for a husking bee," said Betsy.

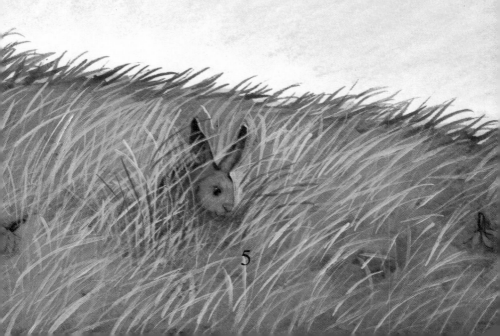

Pap tuned up his fiddle.

Mama sliced a fresh berry pie.

Betsy and her little brother, Judd,

piled corncobs

for the husking contest.

"Look!" said Betsy.

"There's the Dawson wagon."

The wagon pulled up

and Mr. Dawson, Grandma Dawson,

Frank, and the twins jumped down.

"It's so nice to see you!" Mama said.

"We have buffaloberry jam for you."

"Here's a plum pudding,"

Grandma Dawson said.

"Hey, Frank," Judd called,

"let's play tag!"

The boys ran off together.

Betsy watched them go.

She wished she had a friend

to play games with, too.

Mr. and Mrs. Shaw arrived next
from their farm
at Boone Creek Crossing.
"We made candles and have extras
for you," said Mr. Shaw.

The adults talked
about tending their cows and hogs.
The little ones played tag.
Betsy sat alone
making a wildflower necklace
for her corn-husk doll.

Soon Pap called,

"Let's start the husking bee!

We will have two teams.

Everyone pull off the husks

as fast as you can.

Then toss the cobs

onto your team's pile.

The team with the biggest pile

wins all the popped corn

they can eat.

Ready. Set. Go!"

Everyone tugged and pulled.
The corn husks flew this way
and that. The corncob piles grew.

Judd and Frank jumped up.

"Our team won!" they cried.

Betsy didn't care about winning.

All she wanted was a friend.

Chapter 2 ❧ New Folks Are Coming

That night, Mama said,

"I hope we have visitors again soon.

It gets lonely on the prairie."

"Do you think I will ever

have a friend to visit?"

Betsy asked softly.

Pap said, "Mr. Shaw told me

new folks are coming.

Maybe the family

has a daughter your age."

"Can we go meet them?"

Betsy asked.

"Of course," Mama said.

19

A week later, Pap heard

that the new folks had arrived.

Betsy rose early the next day

to go see them,

but a storm came up

and lasted all day and night.

Finally, the sky cleared.

Pap said, "It looks like a fine day

to meet new friends.

I will loan them a pitchfork."

"Take them this loaf of bread

for good luck," Mama said.

Betsy climbed onto the cart.

"Giddyap," Pap said to the horse.

The cart started to roll.

"Suppose there is a girl . . ."
Betsy said. "Sally or Pearl.
Minnie or Flora Belle."

"Those are all nice names,"
said Pap.

At Boone Creek Crossing,

they saw a man

standing by a wagon.

"Welcome," Pap called.

25

"My name is Fitzroy," said the man.

Pap gave Mr. Fitzroy the pitchfork,

and Betsy gave him the bread.

"How kind!" Mr. Fitzroy said.

"My daughter, Emmeline,

is just about your age."

"Emmeline. What a beautiful name!"
Betsy said.

"She's with her mama
back in St. Paul," said Mr. Fitzroy.
"They'll come after I make a dugout
for us to live in."

Pap and Mr. Fitzroy talked about farming.

Betsy thought about catching fish in the creek with Emmeline.

On the ride home, Betsy said,

"I wonder when Emmeline will come."

Chapter 3 ❧ The Corn-Husk Doll

"I am going to make
a corn-husk doll for Emmeline,"
Betsy said the next day.
She put out some husks to dry.

A few days later they were ready.
Betsy gathered them into a bundle,
tied the top, and rounded the head.
It was a good start.

Every day, after her chores,

Betsy worked on the doll.

She braided the arms

and crossed the shoulders.

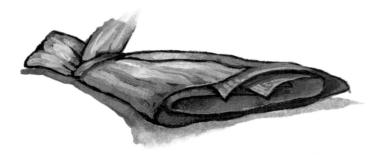

"I want the skirt to be just right,"

Betsy told Mama.

But it turned out flat,

and she had to start over.

This time she used wider husks

and trimmed them

slowly and carefully.

Now the skirt puffed out just right.

"Isn't she pretty!" Mama said.

"I hope Emmeline thinks so,"
said Betsy.

Chapter 4 ❧ A Visit

Betsy and her family
went to Boone Creek Crossing
to help the new family
build a soddy to live in.

At the dugout,
Mr. and Mrs. Fitzroy greeted them.
The Dawsons were there, too.
At last, Betsy saw Emmeline.

Betsy held out the doll.

"This is for you," she said.

Emmeline took it.

She turned it upside down.

She turned it right-side up.

"It's a doll," Betsy said.

"I made her from corn husks."

"I've never seen a prairie doll

before," Emmeline said.

She put the doll down.

Betsy lowered her eyes.

Just then Mama called Betsy over.
"The men are working on the roof.
Grandma Dawson and I
are going to help Mrs. Fitzroy
make a rag rug. Why don't you
and Emmeline go berry picking?"
"I don't think Emmeline likes the doll,"
said Betsy. "I don't think
she wants to be my friend."

"Moving to the prairie is hard

for Emmeline and her family,"

Mama said. "They are city folk.

They need time to learn

about life here,

and they will need our help."

Betsy saw two empty baskets.

"We could have

a berry-picking contest," she said.

"That's a good idea," Mama said.

Betsy said, "Emmeline and I

will be on one team.

Frank and Judd can be on the other."

She told Emmeline about the contest.

"I've never been berry picking,"

Emmeline said.

"I'll show you how," Betsy said.

"I know where to find

berries upstream."

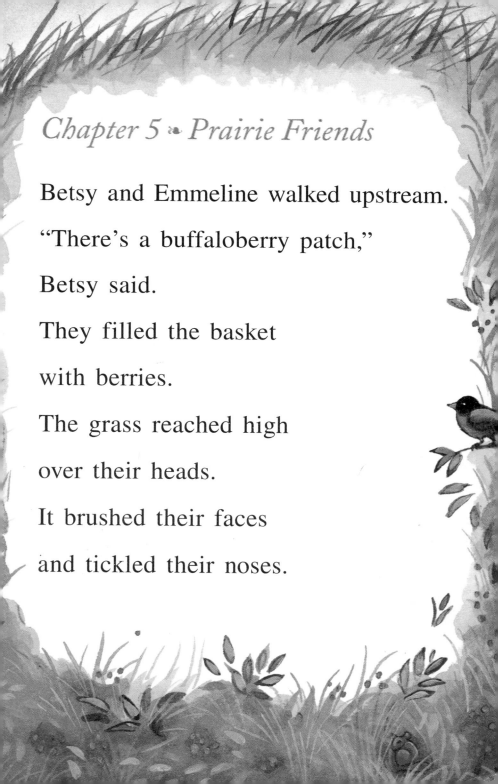

Chapter 5 ☙ Prairie Friends

Betsy and Emmeline walked upstream.

"There's a buffaloberry patch,"

Betsy said.

They filled the basket

with berries.

The grass reached high

over their heads.

It brushed their faces

and tickled their noses.

Soon they were almost done.

Emmeline was very quiet.

Betsy remembered

what her mother had said

about Emmeline's new life

on the prairie.

Betsy took a deep breath and asked, "What are you going to name your doll?"

"I don't know," Emmeline said.

"I used to have a china doll

from a shop. Her name was Ann.

But we had to sell everything

before we came here."

Emmeline sounded like she might cry.

Betsy put down the basket and asked,

"Do you like to play tag?

It's one of my favorite games."

"Mine too," Emmeline said.

"We played it in St. Paul."

"Let's play tag here," Betsy said.

They played tag in the tall grass.

After a while, Betsy said,

"We had better go back now."

She looked around and around.

"The grass is too high.

I can't see the creek," she said.

"Are we lost?" Emmeline asked.

"We have to find the creek

and follow it to your dugout,"

Betsy said.

They went one way,

then another,

but all they saw was grass.

"We are lost!" Emmeline cried.

"What will we do?"

Suddenly Betsy heard something.

Gar-oo-oo. Gar-oo-oo.

"Sandhill cranes!" Betsy said.

"Quick, let's follow their calls!

They land by the creek

at the end of the day."

GAR-OO-OO. GAR-OO-OO.

Betsy and Emmeline

ran after the birds.

Emmeline tripped

and fell in the grass.

Betsy helped her up.

"Don't worry,

we're almost there,"

Betsy said.

They drew closer and closer
to the sound of the cranes.
At last, they saw the creek.
"Now we can find our way home,"
Betsy said.

"You found the way back!

You knew what to do,"

Emmeline said.

"Soon you will, too," Betsy said.

"I will help you learn all about

the prairie."

"Here they come!" everyone cried.

Betsy and Emmeline

ran over to the dugout.

"Where are your berries?"
Judd asked.

"We lost the basket," said Betsy.

"Frank and I won the contest!"
Judd shouted.

Betsy and Emmeline smiled

at each other.

They didn't care about winning.

Emmeline picked up

her new prairie doll.

"I think I'll call her Pearl,"

Emmeline said. "Can you tell me

how you made her?"

Betsy smiled.

"I will show you how,"

she told her new friend.

Author's Note

Pioneers came to America's prairies about one hundred and fifty years ago to farm the land. At first they lived in dugouts, shelters dug into the side of a hill. Later they built one- or two-room soddies by cutting and stacking blocks of earth, called sod, and filling in the spaces with mud. Some people brought simple furniture by wagon. Others made their own tables and chairs from wood and made beds stuffed with corn husks. A soddy was hard to keep clean and could leak when it rained, but it was warm in winter and cool as a cave in summer.

People lived far from one another and often felt lonely. A visit with friends was a special occasion. A visit also allowed people to share food, tools, and other needs like lard or lye for making soap. Families gathered to help one another out. They called the get-togethers "bees." There were planting and harvesting bees, soddy-building and barn-raising bees, quilting bees, apple-picking bees, and corn-husk bees. When the work was done, everyone shared their food in a dinner potluck style—and talked about the next time they might get together.